ALONE

W. MARIE TURKS

Never Alone 139
Palo Alto, California

Library of Congress Card Number: 2003093756
International Standard Book Number: 0-9742349-0-7

Edited by Jessica (Jackley) Flannery
Cover design by Grace Han
Published by Never Alone 139, Palo Alto, California

Additional complimentary copies of this book are available by mail, postage waived,
while publisher supplies last. Refer to Order Form on the last page, or send request
with return mailing information and number of copies requested (up to 3) to the
publisher at address below. To order bulk quantities, send request via email.

Never Alone 139
P.O. Box 50054
Palo Alto, CA 94303
NeverAlone139@aol.com

Printed in the U.S.A. by
Morris Publishing
3212 East Highway 30
Kearney, NE 68847
1-800-650-7888

First Printing, August 2003

In memory of

Arthur F. Quern,
who lived just long enough to impact
profoundly the lives of many,

&

M,
who I wish had chosen to live.

ACKNOWLEDGEMENTS

It still amazes me how I was led to author a book entitled *Alone*, since
so many individuals have been a significant part of my life and living;
some for a reason, a few for a season, and, I hope, the remaining for a
lifetime. Thank you for blessing me with your presence.

Dr. & Mrs. Carlos Eugene Linnear
Abundant Life Christian Fellowship; Kirk & Terri Adams; Alex &
Carmen Adriaanse; Shannon Alexander; Jimmie Alford & Maree
Bullock; Barry & Rhonda (Oliver), & Isaac Applebaum; Teresa
Aquino & Jonathan Ramos; Patti Baker; Norma Barraza; Tony &
Wanda Barsano; Adele Berg; Bill & Marie Bernardy; Ekua Blankson;
Ray & Elaine Blasing; Lawrence Block; Angelene Bonner; Audra
Branstad; David, Patricia, Isaac & Toby Braunstein; Bread of Life;
Rocky & Diane Bridges; Heather Bristol; Andre & Taifa Butler; Katy
Carrel; Joseph Cartharn; Annie Chatman; Jay & Pam Chesavage;
CMU MAMs; William Clinton; Doris Cohen; Rebecca Conway;
Julia Cowan; Isa Darussalum; Chawan De Ramus; Mary Demby;
Mark Dennis; Nicole Dickens; Hanna Djajapranata; Aimee Drolet;
Petra Eggert; Kathy Eminger; Katie Fantin; Ann Farrell; Sam &
Chenel (Van den Berk) Flores; Brian & Corey Franklin; Brad
Fundingsland; Cheryl Gallow; Freddie Gilmore; Mary Sue Gilmore;
Maija Green-Howard; Lori Gould; Lisa Marie Hahn; Jim, Suzie, &
Michael Hall; Tobey & Nancy Hall; Ed & Polly Han; Pyung & Sue
Min Han; Scott & Molly Hansen; Aaron & Heather Harbath;
Charles, Laura & Ben Harris; Darice-Renee' Harris; Tony & Tracy
Harris; Vikki Harris; Curtis Hatamoto; Tracy Heins; Steve Hester &
Family; Mary Hicks; Jeri L. Hill; Trennie Hill; Mike & Ethel Hiraga;
Matthew Hodges; CW, Evelyn, & Erin Hooi; Lynne Hoppe; Maria
Hyler; Joel Ishler; Veronica Jackson; Wayne & Elise Jackson; The
Johnson Family; Darlene Johnson; Katrina Johnson; Adriene Jones;
George & Janet (Gordon) Kennedy; Merle Khoo; Karin
Kurio; Andrew & Janet Lederer; Loma Linda University Children's
Hospital; Andy, Rosie (Kasim) Aishah & Hamzah Maas;

v

Philippa Marsh; Bob, Olena & Max Marshall; Dan J. Martin; Michael D. Martin; Louie Martirez; Bob & Anne Masheris; Alissa Mathison; Daneen Matts; Ilene Meeks; Phil & Martha (Chavez) McGivney; Trish McLeod; Timothy & Sharon Miller; Ria Monroe; NEA Arts Admin Fellows; Jeff Nerdin & Michelle Schneiter; New Creation Home Ministries Girls; Rosemarie Nola; Anya Nkyforiak; Antonio & Micaela Ochoa; Micaela V. Ochoa; Niall O'Connor; Cynthia Ohanian; Kathleen Park; Patti Cotton Pettis; Bernard Poirier & Family; Jan Polnoff; John & Jee Yoon Ponyicsanyi; Wendy Powell; John & Susannah (Quern) Pratt; Patti Quarrels; Jacqueline Quern; Margaret Quern; DeWayne Quinn; Dean Rally & Family; Hyo, Karen (Kernosek), Nathan & Isabella Rhee; Renate Riendl; Tippi Rivera; Lanson & Gloria Robinson; Nettie Robinson; Winnie Robinson; Olivia Rodriguez; Marilyn Rogowski; Linda Rosenblum; Ingrid Rowland; Ron & Alison Saiki; Steve, Diana (Adamic) & Tia Salika; Yasmin Santiago; Faye Saunders; Mark Scalzo & Family; Carolyn Schwarzkopf; Jill Sewill; Payal Sharma; Sharon Sheehan; Paul & Meredith Sheppard; Lorena Shih; Joseph Strance; The Amsterdam Stranger; Linda Sullivan; Bethany Swain; Bernard Tagholm; Gary & Maria Taylor; Rene' Taylor; The Turks Family; Rebecca Turks; Samuel Turks; Samuel, Sophia, Jean & Sasha (Martin), LaShay (Sakaria), & Sammy Turks; Verlonzo Turks; Jim Valko & Mary Scarvada; Vikki Van Sooy; Elsa Villanueva; Joan Walls; Robin Walls; Karen Weatherill; Richard Wee & Family; Jennifer Wiedel; Victoria Wells; Monico Whittington; Payson & Linda Wild; Cindy Williams; Jackie Williams; Ronne' Wingate; Leigh Wolf ; Kristin Wood; Melvin Wynn; Tammy Yaeger; Genevieve Yirenkyi; and to all the world's angels disguised as librarians.

Undying gratitude to Gail Johnson and Lisa Powell for graciously reviewing my manuscript; Julianne "Hope" Leibsohn for helping me to live it out way before and during composition; Jessica (Jackley) Flannery for editing the book as if she were indeed the smarter half of my brain; and Grace Han for designing the book cover, being the constant friend, and getting it all started with an invitation to go for a walk.

CHAPTERS

PART ONE: EVERYDAY

PART TWO: EVERMORE

Where can I go from your Spirit? Where can I flee from your presence? If I go up to the heavens, you are there; if I make my bed in the depths, you are there. If I rise on the wings of the dawn, if I settle on the far side of the sea, even there your hand will guide me, your right hand will hold me fast. If I say, "Surely the darkness will hide me and the light become night around me," even the darkness will not be dark to you; the night will shine like the day, for darkness is as light to you.

Psalm 139: 7-12
NIV

PART ONE

EVERYDAY

LOST

Before I was born, I lived in a womb. I existed inside another person. I was inside her and with her. We were two. We were one. I was not alone.

I listened to the world with muted ears. I touched the outside from behind her wall. Though it tried, the outside never touched me, because I was safe and secure inside my mother's every breath, sight, and movement. Every pore of me was inside another being. That was then.

At the moment of my birth, I was forced to breathe in the world on my own. I was alone and exposed to everything and everyone. No longer protected, I wailed.

One night when I was twelve, I wrapped myself in a cocoon of blankets to mimic the warmth and security of my mother's womb. There in the quiet, I found another, deeper place inside. This inside was not within another person. It was inside of me.

I had found the place inside myself where I saw me from both inside and outside. Like seeing an inner layer of myself from the innermost layer. In this place, I was looking in, and looking out, and looking in. I was seeing nothing and seeing everything.

This place was my core. It was without sound, color, touch, scent, memory, and language. These things did not exist there, instead, there they were conceived. It was difficult for me to understand how nothing, but my entirety, was there in nucleic, no, molecular form. Perhaps this place was the center of my spirit, or the essence of my soul.

Whatever it was, it scared me.

In that place, my will, my thoughts, and my intuition lay unborn again. There were no facades, no perceptions, or fragments. There was pure me: raw, void, and solitary.

My visit there seemed like hours, but probably lasted a couple of minutes. I cannot tell you for certain because in my center, I stood outside of time.

At that acute moment, I believed if I stayed within any longer, returning to my outer life would be impossible. I would remain inside watching myself, obsessed with the view. I would spend the rest of my life treading in a veritable Bermuda triangle, sinking inside my tide, bound to an internal anchor, held without hands, left without faculties in a pre-natal sea of nothingness. I would lie trapped within my embryonic core, wanting to escape, but never able to leave it behind.

In that place, my nascent personhood would exist at least two degrees away from the rest of humanity. No one could ever see, touch, or know me. Sure, I might have a physical presence and function in the moving world. But living trapped at the beginning of my being, I would be experientially separated from life, casting a mere reflection for others to see from an empty distance.

Fearing separation from life as I knew it, I vowed to exist outside of that place. It is inside of me, it is everywhere I go: it is everything I am, yet to it, I refused to go. Returning to that place meant birth and death, so I stayed away from me. And I chose to live in the medium between my core and the outer world. Alone and scared of being alone, I hid.

In desperate attempt to hide from myself, as I grew older, I lost myself in activities and addictions. I went to crowded places, looking for safety in congregations, using the masses for protection. I sought to vanish in the multitude of people rather than in the tide of myself.

When I spent nights alone, I watched TV, listened to music, organized my mail, and talked on the phone — sometimes, all four at once — did anything so as not to be still. I knew if my surroundings were quiet, the echoes of my inner solitude would deafen me.

Going through life, I also learned as while I hid from that place, I had the ability to hide things there I wanted to forget. Safe into the Bermuda waters of pre-me, things such as pain, scars, irreconcilable differences, and consequential indifferences were thrown and kept there, shackled to the bottom of my unfathomable internal sea. They were gone, but somehow never forgotten.

As my attempts to hide intensified, so did the craving to know more about myself. In my search, the same as when I was hiding, I sought to reside in the company of people. I was looking for someone to tether me as I walked to the edge of the place and peered inside. I hoped with them there, I might uncover a path to my inside, and also find a way back to everyday living.

Then at one point, I glimpsed a reflection of the place from the outside when I saw a candid photograph of myself. That photo revealed the real me who was caught off-guard and frozen inside a still-life frame. Intrigued, I began to search for real-time, candid reflections of me in store-front windows when I went out alone. I also went to movies, restaurants, parks, and other solitary places, hoping to find another shadow of my core.

Finally, in an effort to circumvent my conflicted state of hide-and-seek, I slept every chance I got, where, for a short time, I divorced myself from the relentless struggle. While sleeping, I pretended I was unborn again, protected, and united. Sleep became my escape, a temporary suspension. Sleep, however, did not shelter me: the part of me that hid and sought often wailed and woke me from slumber into alarm. So the struggle continued.

In spite of my hide and search efforts, Truth declared I was alone. It mocked me and pointed out that my hiding attempts fertilized my restlessness. It also said if I went to my core, whether in a crowd or by myself, isolation would haunt me. If I looked within, thought, or even sat still, no one would be there at my center. Truth said, that even if I found someone willing to join me in the place, they could not enter. In and with everything, I was a lone soul.

Truth explained, if my stark core were exposed for the world to see, how could anyone know the whole of me, the none of me? Who could live in the birthplace of my thoughts, my will, my emotion, and my intuition at every moment, every day of my entire life? No one. I conceded to my absolute impenetrability. And I loathed it.

With concession, Truth stabbed me with the realization that if I have an impenetrable core, everyone has an impenetrable core: we can not experience each other at our places of being. Whatever our strength, even if we opened every door and tore down every wall, I could not incorporate another person any more than they could me. We could wade through the watered-logged layers of our personas, but never meet each other at the depths of our cores.

Truth reminded me of our impenetrable centers whenever I gazed outside my bedroom window to watch life in motion. I watched the sun transforming the sill's spider-webs into fine threads of gold. I watched falling water rain color and release fragrances from the trees and flowers. I watched the ever-changing wind stir the leaves into an air dance. But whenever I reached out to experience the sun, rain, and wind, the window blocked my hand. I saw energy and action, but I was unable to touch its core. So I wondered if what I was seeing, through the glass, even existed. Was anything I saw real?

Truth, via that window to the moving world, illustrated how I am locked out and locked in. Others cannot touch the real me, nor can I touch them. And perhaps, like me, others are lost within themselves, running from and looking for their inside. Every person is alone. This thought scared me even more.

Today, I am still scared.

I remain lost, frozen outside of my core. I think many of the answers I need might even be found there since my core is the place before the questions began. Yet, I have chosen to reside in this wilderness called "everyday life" where I am sustained, but I am not thriving in an idyllic land.

I am terrified that I will spend my life in a predictable, inescapable, hide-and-seek cycle of looking in places, pursuing all things, and using everyone. And I fear that, all the while, I will know I am destined to live inside this forest of fear, trapped between the core of my being and living.

How ironic! I was conceived in physical union and existed for a while in a womb. Today, I live buried alive, hiding, searching, and lost in an isolated tomb.

ALONE

AIRBORNE

I smile, sometimes. I get mad, sometimes. I laugh, sometimes. I get sad a lot. Most of the time though, I wonder if I died, would anybody miss me?

How long before someone found me, or found me missing? What would they remember about me? How many months or years until I was forgotten? Who would wear my shoes, carry my identity, use my keys, and own my soul? Maybe if I hadn't left home, things would have been better.

Sometimes, I wish I were dead.

I'm sure everybody will be better-off when I die. Nobody needs or knows me anyway; I don't even know myself. Like why do I get upset over stupid stuff, and why do I hate spiders? Why do I spend so much time wondering about what might have been?

Here comes a spider now. I'm going to kill it.... I wonder if it knew today was its day to die? Did it know my next step meant its last darkness?

I see darkness everywhere. Signs of the so-called times: *Beware of Dog. Beware of Cat. Beware of Children. Keep off Grass. Don't Walk. Vista Closed at Sunset. Street Closed to Thru Traffic. No Parking. No Public Restrooms. No Loitering. No Diving. No Wading Allowed.* Quick, someone arrest those ducks!

I drive. I walk. I do the "Don'ts" and "No-s". Since when have there been hours for looking at the Vista anyway?

Most signs I don't even notice anymore. I just do what they say like everybody else. We obey *Don't Walk* without thinking, we never realize we're idling, jammed, merely waiting for the *Walk* sign to flash us back into vitality. Look at that guy, jogging in place at the red light, so sad. Why doesn't he jog across to the opposite sidewalk if he wants to keep moving? Okay... one moooore second... okay... green light, and he's off! People are idiots.

Everything everywhere is an admonition, a limit, a don't-do. They might as well say don't live. With all these stupid signs, nobody has a reason to. Especially me. Everything I do, everywhere I go leads to one, larger-than-life sign flashing *No!* I'm tired of waiting, getting my hopes up, and running into *No.* Why is everything a struggle against everything when it doesn't matter in the end anyway? Nothing ever does.

I wonder what would happen if I drove into a tree? What if I walked across the freeway at midnight when the trucks rent the road? Or, what if I stabbed myself? Maybe I'll drink some Liquid Plumber® and let it dissolve me from the inside.

How long does it take to drown, surrendering to the ocean's swell while it rips me from the shore of existence? If I drown, I don't want anybody to find me. Maybe somebody will find me. I long to die. Oh, but wait a minute, I forget, *No Diving.*

There's this tree-lined street near my house that runs parallel to a dry creek. I drive about 10 mph on that street because the road is full of potholes. I don't know why but somehow, I identify with those potholes.

I should drive a little faster. I've only got about 20 minutes to get home and re-dress. I wish I didn't have to go out, I'd rather be alone. I'm so tired of the game and putting on the "face." I'm tired of talking about the good 'ole days that seem good because we remember them while we drink beer. I wonder if this is the night when somebody will give me a reason. Can anybody explain anything?

Sometimes I want to fly above everything to see the answers from a bird's-eye view. Is it me, or does it seem like there are a lot of birds walking around lately? Why are they walking, when they have wings? Probably a sign up there somewhere telling them *Don't Fly*. I see them pecking around, gathering sticks and string for their nests. How do they decide where to build a nest anyhow...some place high, some place quiet, some place with running water? How can birds do so much without hands? Never mind. It's just another thing for no one to explain.

Music rocks the night, and laughter peals from far away; noises are everywhere and I don't hear a thing. The earth swirls and I am at the edge, finally, with a bird's-eye view. I'll be a bird. I will build a nest someplace high. Forget about the signs, I'm going to spread my wings and fly....

It feels good to soar. The wind screams into my soul. I don't have any more questions. But I hear screams rushing at my back. I want to fly back to their voices. Wait! I don't want to land! I am a bird. I belong in the sky. I want to know.

No one knew. I should have told them I only wanted to fly. But with a step, I died.

ALONE

TRUCKIN'

The story of my life takes a whole lifetime to tell. I already lived it, so I ain't got much to say.

I left home at 16. I got lost, so I ran. Didn't know where I was goin'. Just headed for someplace that wasn't home.

When I got tired of runnin', I started drivin': trucks. I seen it all and I been everywhere with my hands on the wheel. I seen mountains, lakes, and fields. I seen cows, sheep, and horses grazin' on the sides. I seen sunsets, sunrises, and rainbows in every color.

There's a lotta beauty on the road. Sometimes it don't seem real, seems like I'm drivin' in a paintin' somebody painted. I make believe it's all a mere paintin', else the beauty is too painful to take in.

Yep, I own the road. It's where I live. I got my bed in the back, fur on the mirror, and a map on the dash. That's everythin' I need.

I think about my family sometimes and wonder if they miss me. They didn't know me, so I guess they don't miss me. I'm alright on my own.

I drive mostly at night 'cuz I like havin' the road to myself. When I see somebody drivin' a car late at night, I honk my horn and it scares the daylights out of 'em. I get a kick outta that.

I ran away when I was 16. Only problem is, I came with me.

ALONE

Lookout

I'm always standing, except when I can sit.

> I protect. I make things secure, not people.
> I'm important. If you don't need me, I've done my job.
> I spend most nights in office buildings, alone.
> Reading. Thinking. Wondering. Being. And I get paid for it.
> I'm always looking in, even when I'm looking out.

ALONE

CRUMB

I'm everywhere but you don't see me, even when I'm in front of you.

You don't know my name. I know yours.

I know what you ate, what you didn't, what you wrote, what you used and what you didn't want. I know all about your crumbs.

I take out your trash. I clean your office. I help you forget. Some things you should remember.

When I'm around, the place is near empty, but my bags are near full.

I have friends. I have a family and I do have a name. It's Evangelina.

ALONE

LOIT

Everywhere is my home, but I can't find a heart. I fight for everything I have, which is nothing. I hate when it rains.

You see me, but pretend you don't. I disgust you. You won't dare look me in the eye. You afraid I might somehow see you looking at me with shame. You the one who's ashamed, I'm not. You afraid I might say something to you, or tell you my story. You don't want to hear my story. That's okay 'cuz I don't want to tell it, don't need to. How I got here makes no difference, because I am here. I'm here now. Keep on walking.

You think I want to be like you. You think I want your house, your car, your friends, and your job. You always got someplace to go, somewhere to be. You go to places you don't even want to go to. I don't. I don't even know what day it is and I don't care. What do I have to do? I don't care about time either. You see that sun shining up there? It blinds me to the hour. What time is it? Why do I need to know the time? I already got plenty of it.

I don't want to be you. You can keep your purse, lady. I don't want your things. I got everything I need right here in my bags where I can see 'em, hold 'em, and get at 'em when I need to. I like what's in my bags; anything you got is junk to me.

You think I want money, a handout. I could get a job, you know, but why? You don't like your job. I hear you talking. Me, I collect cans. There's no money in it; it's not a job, it gives me something to do. And I like the way the cans sound. Plus, you hear me coming, and you stop to look at me. Besides, what would I do with money, spend it...save it...eat it...drink it...smoke it...lose it? I don't need options or choices.

Instead of your handout, how about your hand? Wanna shake my hand? I bet you don't. You afraid they might tell you my story. You afraid you might have to touch the hours, days, and years I've lived on the street. I'll give you the time of day. You look like you need a handout.

Got kicked off the street this morning. Man pointed to a sign that said, *No Loitering*. That's another way of saying you gotta have someplace else to go if you wanna be here. I got no place to go so they say I loiter. What else is there to do? Just call me Loit. You never ask me my real name anyway. Haven't heard my name said in a while. Tomorrow, I will write it down in nice big letters, carry it around, and look at it every now and then to remind myself who I am. Gotta be careful not to lose the paper with my name on it, though. On second thought, forget about it. It'd be just another thing I gotta carry. Just call me Loit.

When I need a bathroom I come to the library. I used to sit outside on the grass all day, all the time. My old spot is just dirt now. So I had to leave, moved on to greener pastures. I still sit there sometimes, just to have someplace to go, where I used to be. I couldn't tell you my story if I wanted to cause you gotta be quiet in the library.

What I do here is look at books. My vision's not so good, but I can see pictures. Glasses got stolen by some other streeter when I was sleeping. Or maybe it was a critter, or some brats. Kids think things is funny and they like to play around. One day a stray dog got a lot of their attention. He wagged his tail, he barked, he chased a stick. One kid took him home. Tomorrow, I'll try barking. I could look for some more glasses, but what is there to see but people who don't want to see me? No, thanks, blurry pictures is fine. At least they look like they're looking at me.

In the library, sometimes I force myself to look in the mirror. My hair is dirty. My eyes are red. Eyebrows are grey. There's things in my beard which don't belong there. Leave 'em alone in their little wilderness on my face. I try not to look at myself in the mirror too much, just long enough to remind me what I used to look like. I still got that mole. There's nothing much else there I want to see. Since I can't do a whole lot about what I see staring back at me, why look too hard?

Yeah, I know you think I stink. I see you making faces, turning up your nose on the street when I pass by. You're clean, I know. But hot water don't work here. Cold water runs thin. Soap don't do a whole lot for me anymore and I stopped being able to smell my stink a long time ago, so I don't care. It's not my problem.

My teeth are rotting. I don't have a brush. I don't need one. My teeth will all be gone soon, won't need a brush then. Before they invented toothbrushes, everybody around had teeth like mine. That's why no one's smiling in those old pictures I see in the art books. You won't need a brush either, one day. Meantime, just one more thing to carry I don't need. I gotta travel light.

My shoes. Of course you didn't notice them. You too busy looking at yours when you walked past me. My shoes got secrets. Yeah, they don't match. They don't even fit. In fact, if you looked real hard you'd see they're barely there. They overrun their miles and the foundations are weak. And the bottom of my feet are so tough, I didn't notice one of my shoes had a hole in it, and that the other one was missing half its sole. I'm like the both of them rolled up into one neat package; half of my soul got a hole in it too.

I wear all the clothes I own. I put them on in layers. It's easier that way to find something when I need it.

Sometimes, before I leave the bathroom, I flick the lights when no one else is around. I act like it's my bathroom, my electricity. Nowhere else I can go with switches I can touch.

I eat what I can find, what you don't want. A squirrel beat me to your leftovers the other day. He probably buried 'em in the ground somewhere. I wonder if he remembers where. I wanna follow him and get 'em back.

ALONE

I sleep where I can, where you won't bother me. My favorite spot is in the dry creek when the water is low. I make my bed on the rocks and I look up and listen. Sometimes kids come by with their bicycles. It's not the smoothest street up there. It's full of potholes so very few cars drive by. Those that do drive by real slow so as not to blow out a tire and end up over the edge. Then they'd land here right next to me, at the bottom.

Yeah, inside, down in the creek is my secret place. It's right nice. I'm here on the inside, outside of your world, right where I belong.

TWO

We love each other and have a great life. We met when we were in school. We had the same goals. We laughed at the same things. We have successful lives and lots of interests. We have our home and we have each other.

"How can I tell her that this isn't my dream?"
" I wish he'd tell me my dreams matter."

"I work hard, for you. I thought that's what you wanted."
"I work because I don't have you. You are what I wanted."

"You don't know me. Only what you want me to be."
"I don't know you. You don't know me either, how could you love me? "

"I'm afraid of failing. Then you'd see I'm not who I promised I'd be."
"I am hurting. Can't you see?"

"Why won't you let me in? I can't get past you, your walls."
"You are here, but you're so far away. Where are you?"

"I miss us."

"I need you to hold me. See me. Sometimes I want to be cradled in your arms, like a child."

"Maybe if I touch you, you will see me."
"Come be with me; don't solve me, just love me.

"Tell me I'm your hero."
"Tell me I'm your jewel."

"Tell me you need me."
"Tell me you want me."

"You touch me but you don't feel me."
"My hands touch you and feel nothing."

"Inside you I fall into the depths of my loneliness."
"With you inside only emptiness grows."

"Two is a lonely number."
"Two is a lonely number."

We've had our share of problems. Most of our friends have separated, but we're still together. After all this time, we're still together. They are not.

TRYING

I'm a single mom and I'm tired.

I have 3 kids, all boys. They're great, but it's a tough job.

My husband left. He said it was too much for him. If it was too much with the both us, did he think it'd be easier for me, by myself?

My kids are good company. I'm never alone. They always need something like tissues, milk, or Superman. I wish there were more of me to go around. Everyday, I'm trying.

I love them so much. I love them best when they're asleep. Then, I listen for a cough, a sneeze, or a scream. With boys, if it's too quiet something is wrong.

Sometimes I have to go into the bathroom to get some time alone. I can usually get about 40 seconds. That's when I sleep.

ALONE

EMPTY

I waited to have a child. When I was ready to conceive, I discovered I was infertile.

Others don't want their kids. They ignore them, leave them, or kill them.

There are no wet eyelashes, runny noses, or finger-paintings in my home. There are no peanut butter sandwiches in the VCR, bars of soap in the fishbowl, or car keys in the toilet. Our house is clean and it's quiet, all the time.

Give me your child. I would hold his hand, every time I had the chance. I would smell his hair, nibble his feet, and watch him while he slept. I've got enough love. I know I do.

Ours is a good home. We love each other. But we put off having a child and our backyard is still empty, like me.

ALONE

DARK

I'm black. I'm not African-American. I don't identify with Africa.

Everyone else is white: Caucasian, Asian, Latino, Indian, Polynesian — it doesn't matter. You're all white to me.

I stand out. I'm constantly spotted in a crowd. I'm the dark spot. Have you ever been a spot?

You like me. You think I'm nice and you get to know me.

You wonder about me. How did I get into that school? What does my hair feel like? Do I tan? Believe it or not, I am intelligent. You can touch it. And no, I don't need to tan, I'm already dark.

When I see other spots, we smile at each other for no reason, and for every reason.

I like to dance. Don't you?

Sorry, I don't know a whole lot about my last name. No, I don't know its origin. My family tree doesn't have any roots.

I work, I laugh, I kiss, I forget, I cry, I hope, I bleed — exactly like you.

But I'm black. You're not.

ALONE

AVERAGE

I'm just your average guy. I get up every morning, get dressed, have a cup of coffee, kiss my wife, hug my kids, take out the trash, and I go to work — the same route every day.

My job is a job. I'm not passionate about it. It's a decent living, and it pays the bills. I'm putting my kids through school, and paying off the house. I try to take a vacation with the family every year. The kids seem to like camping.

We have birthdays, reunions, and barbeques. I watch football on Monday nights. On Wednesday mornings, I golf with the guys.

Sometimes I wonder what my life might have been, if I didn't get married, or didn't have kids, or didn't have this job? Where would I be now?

My entire life, I have heard people talk about a calling. They seem to wake up with a passion for the day and look forward to seizing their tomorrows. I have never had a calling, other than a call to be on time for dinner.

I love my wife, she understands me and she knows exactly what I need, even when I don't.

My kids, they are great but they have their own things.

My home is comfortable, and my neighborhood is safe. I have provided for my family, I've done my job.

But I can't help wondering what else is out there. I wonder what it feels like to be free from the weight of an ordinary life. There has got to be more than this, but maybe there isn't. And if there is, I must have missed it. In that case, it's better not to even think about it.

Anyway, I've got a mortgage to pay, mouths to feed, and a lawn to water. No use thinking about what might have been.

Six o'clock again, time to go home. Dinner will be waiting, my kids will be on the Internet, and my wife will be asking questions. Did I remember to pick up a loaf of French bread? Yeah, I remembered. Maybe one day someone will ask me about something more than dinner.

Tonight, I think I'll take the long way home.

DRAWBACK

I live alone. There is no one here but me. There are no pets, no plants. There's just me, and I like it.

When I come home at night, everything is exactly as I left it in the morning. Nothing has been moved. Nothing moves. Everything is where it belongs. What more could I ask for?

Other people wish they were like me because I do everything how I want it done. I go where I want. I eat what I want. I sleep when I want. I laugh at my own jokes. I answer to no one. No one answers to me. The shoes at the door are all the same size: mine. No one needs anything from me. No one bothers me. I hear no other voices but my own. I have no commitments. There is no one I have to trust and no one I have to worry about disappointing. No one's coming home. No one's leaving. I love it.

I cook for one. I like my own company. When I'm bothered by anything I don't like about myself, I've got books to tell me how to make myself better.

I don't read much. But I do lots of other things. I have lots of hobbies. I like to travel. I have been everywhere. You can cover a lot of ground on your own. When you're alone in a crowd, it's easier to disappear and keep moving.

I do like to watch TV when I'm home alone. I especially like it when the TV is still on when I wake up.

I like going to the movies by myself sometimes too. It's like I'm in a private conversation with the actors on the screen. They tell me their stories.

I do have some family and lots of friends. When I want to talk, I phone them. And I leave a message.

Most of my friends have their own families. I spend time with them some nights. It's great and we have lots of fun. When the fun is over, I go home.

They suggest I find someone, settle down, and have a family of my own. But it's difficult to find the right type of person. I'm not picky, just selective. What's wrong with that? I'm looking for someone with the basics: attractive, employed, smart, outgoing, mature, fun to be around, and honest. Well, I'd have to say, someone like me, who adores me. Know anybody?

Since I'm alone, I don't have to answer the door when someone knocks. I can keep the curtains closed, turn off everything, and pretend nobody's home.

When I want it quiet, I make it quiet. My neighbor has 3 kids and her place is noisy. Often, there's a sneeze, a laugh, a cough, or a song over there. I'm glad I'm over here, where it's mellow. That's how I like it.

The best part about living alone? Sleeping in on Saturday mornings! I woke up today at 11 a.m. I left home at 2 p.m. I went out for a late lunch and had my own table, ordered what I wanted. Placing my order, I spoke the first words I said out loud today.

There is only one drawback to living alone — I can't reach my back when it itches. I have to stand against the corner of my wall to scratch, or find a hairbrush, or a clothes-hanger. I hate that.

And it's never really all that quiet here. Sounds from the outside seep in; the wind rustles the leaves, trucks honk from the street, and birds chirp at the crack of dawn. Those birds are always chirping. Dawn, it's always cracking.

Inside, the refrigerator hums all the time; even when it's empty.

Other people wish they were like me. I don't know why. I do everything how I want it done. I go where I want. I eat what I want.

I sleep when I want. I laugh at my own jokes. I answer to no one. No one answers to me. The shoes at the door are all the same size: mine. No one needs anything from me. No one bothers me. I hear no other voices but my own. I have no commitments. There is no one I have to trust and no one I have to worry about disappointing. No one's coming home. No one's leaving.

When I come home at night, everything is exactly as I left it in the morning. Nothing has been moved. Nothing moves. Everything is where it belongs.

I live alone. There is no one here but me.

ALONE

GRUMPS

My wife died 7 years ago. I died then too.

Parts of me live on, though. My son and grandsons look like me when I was young. They run around, go camping, and play baseball — but they don't visit me much.

They say I smell bad, and that they don't like my teeth. So I keep them in a jar. What's wrong with my teeth? I got the best my money could buy.

I had a good life. I worked for years to get to where I am now: alone, here in this place they call a home.

We're all alone, together. But we've got the memory of our memories to keep us company.

ALONE

WHISPERS

Me here 3 week. Me here 6 week too soon.

Me skin thin. Me cold quick. Me air no work. Nooduls in me. Big faces ove me, say 'tie-nee' all time. Dat my name? Faces say it soft.

Nose by me has nooduls too. Nose by me has red line go up and low. Nose by me has big faces dat rain. No faces rain ove me.

Me get soft words, no rain.

Me too wee to rain ove.

ALONE

PHAT

I'm Fat. At first I was Healthy. Then I was Big-Boned. Next was Heavy. Then came Overweight. Later it was Morbidly Obese. Today, I overheard that it's official...the judges have declared me hands-down, Horizontally-Unchallenged!

But I prefer plain old fat, in lower-case letters. It's simple and it's the truth. Those three letters are the smallest thing about me. At least there is something small about me.

You see me and think BIG, but you don't know the half-n-half of it. Every movement makes me sweat. With all the sweating you'd think I'd lose a pound or ten. Everything and everyone seems so far away. I'm an island unto myself. It's impossible for me get away from it all, because my all is everywhere.

You all seem so happy and thin, walking around in the latest fashions, showing your bare waistlines wasting away, sipping lattes, and whining about how you overdosed on a bag of baby carrots over Thanksgiving. Gimme a break! Or at least gimme some chocolate. You want to see a waistline? How about this S.S. Waist-liner where my belly-button will remind you of a fat, jolly, jelly donut to go with that latte of yours.

Nothing fits me, not my clothes, not my shoes — not me. I can't find a fashionable print in my size that doesn't make me look like a walking sofa. And yes, that mysterious swishing sound you hear when

I walk is, in fact, the sound of my thighs rubbing together. I can't get daylight to shine between them when I stand, but ask me to walk around the block and the friction between my legs will start a bonfire to flare up your life.

Walking is work. And when it gets really bad, and people start staring, I put my hand on my lower back and I say that I'm pregnant with triplets. People start holding doors open for me and asking me if I know what I'm having. Yeah, two identical Big Mac® sandwiches and one Über-size fries, to-go! Oh yeah, and don't forget the Diet Coke®.

And I'll tell you something else: fat is not free! After Gram Watchers, Slim not-so-Fast, Fat-Busting, Sugar-Bashers, Metabosize, Liquidator, hypnosis, acupunct-me, blue algae, green tea, and low-carb, I've spent so much dough on diets, I think I'll market a new one: "How to Lose Your Big Fat Mind!" One more diet and there will be nothing left to eat, or not to eat. I might as well eat what I want. Maybe all the food will cancel itself out.

Remember a few years ago when the word "phat" was popular? It meant great, cool, and awesome, sort of like when the word "bad" was dubbed to mean "good". I got the letters P-H-A-T put on sweatshirt once and wore it to a modern art exhibit. I was art-in-motion big time, a walking ton-o'-pun. It wasn't much longer before phat vanished; I guess someone saw me coming. Of course, they saw me coming, I'm all over the place. I wish I were phat. And, I want to disappear like phat did. Maybe if I sang, it would all be over.

When you're fat, people think you smell bad too. I see their faces when I sit down or walk by. They expect me to stink. I don't: do I? I can't tell. My nose can't smell around all of me.

YESIHAVETRIEDGOINGTOTHEGYM!!!

They refused to sell me a pass, little wonder. The excuse...? They ran out of open spaces for new members — meaning, there was no space for someone with an abyss like mine. I'm so grrrreat at being great, I over-achieved their maximum weight requirements! The gym belongs exclusively to the thin.

My all-time favorite remark is when someone tells me I have such a pretty face — in that patronizing, bewildered tone, like they dare not look any lower to comment on my girlish figures. Please somebody just sew my mouth shut and give me a sheet to wear and make it queen-sized. It could save us both tons of energy. You won't have to look at me and I won't have to try. You're not looking at my clothes anyway, just my pretty face.

Social life? Like my clothes, I have outgrown my friends; big surprise, right? Not many places I can go by myself these days and fit in.

Restaurants? I can't go out to eat because the seats are too small. And I can't eat without other people glaring at me, in particular, those sitting by themselves. Their eyes constantly tell me I need a bigger table and that I don't need the mayo.

Buses? I can't take them because the bus drivers don't want to wait for me to climb the steps. Soon, I'll need to trade in my car for a SUB. When I drive this one, truckers honk and other drivers look at me like I'm strangling a small animal.

Libraries are nice, though. They have enough room, and in the art books, I see how a real female body is supposed to look. Some paintings have big women in them. Not big like me, but at least not so small like the rest of you. I hate you.

And I hate arm-rests, crowded places, picnics on the grass, seat belts, side salads, public toilets, panty hose, zippers, and scales. But most of all, I hate mirrors.

I do, however, love elastic.

ALONE

ADDICTED

Every morning I have a cup of comfort and consciousness. I do love coffee — the way it smells, the way it tastes, and what it does for me.

I relish sitting alone in the corner of a café, as every sip of clarity filters today's to-do items into tomorrow's possibilities.

I don't need it. I'm not addicted. I can change to decaf anytime I want. But I don't really like decaf, it's too weak.

So what? Everybody needs a vice. I'm not perfect and I'm not alone.

ALONE

CHARMED

I'm a student in the school of life.

There is so much to learn. There are plenty of things out there leading me down the wide path to genuine wealth, love, and happiness. I've done it all — the conferences, the retreats, the treasure hunts, the books, the cards, the crystals, the colors, the incense, and the tea leaves — and I have learned from the best.

The people who lecture and write, they're the experts, they know it all. They are knowledgeable and learned, like me. They are people, just like me.

Besides, if I don't get the answers in this lifetime, I can come back to life as something else and live life over again. And again. And again.

Those experts, they'll be here too, barking out the precise moment in time they think I've lived my life right.

ALONE

BLIND

Where I'm from, there was war, hunger, and death everyday. I saw it.

My father was shot dead right before my eyes. A soldier tortured and killed my mother, and I was forced to watch. One of my eyes was blinded during an explosion at school. Later, they took my brother away and I haven't seen him since.

A neighbor helped me escape and I'm now looking out from the boat that's taking me to a new place. He says I'll have a new life there, with lots of new things to do and see.

It might be a good place, but with my family gone now, I'm an orphan. There's nothing there I want to see because there's no one left with eyes like mine.

ALONE

DNR

I'm ill. I'm very ill. I could die at any moment. In fact, I think I died once already. They brought me back to life. What for?

I've lived a good life. Most of my family and friends are dead already, and I envy them. But they left me here to live alone with my pain, my pills, and the wait. Each day it gets more difficult waiting for death, never knowing where or when, but hoping it will be soon.

Once, I was almost there, almost free, almost taken, almost gone. But they refused to let me die. They brought me back to life. I wish they hadn't.

I won't almost die again. See this? It's a DNR form. DNR means "Do Not Resuscitate." I don't want your air. Do not breathe into me. I have had enough of living and breathing. Breathing means pain.

I carry my DNR everywhere I go, just in case, so everyone knows they've got my permission to let my breaths die.

So if my heart stops ticking on your watch, please, just let me die. I have had enough. I don't want to breathe if I have a choice when the time comes. In fact, don't even bother to ask me. Just let me die.

ALONE

OVERSHADOWED

My universe is silence – sounds without echoes, breaths without air, sights without color, touch without love. I am living with you through every moment, in subordinate witness to everything you experience and behold. My eternity dwells in the whispers of your life.

I hear all of your secrets. Anything you want to know, ASK ME!

I know everything about you. I know what you're doing right now. I have gone where you've gone. I am with you where you go. You are not alone. Your every step is my step. Where you go, there I AM!

I've been here and you've been here, but we've been strangers. Maybe one day you will EMBRACE ME!

You believe each person is one-of-a-kind, with a matchless set of fingerprints, a unique scent, and inimitable thoughts. You say you are alone. Don't you know everything you are I am, and everything I am is you? We are two and we are one. KNOW ME!

Every day I am beside you, behind you, in front of you, within and without, carrying you, knowing you, and believing in you. I am the evidence of your existence, but you refuse to SEE ME!

How long must I wait in this realm of absent reflection? Look in the light...a rabbit, a giraffe, anything...just ENLIVEN ME. Without you, I am nothing but a lonely shadow, in the dark.

ALONE

ALONE

To know me, think of yourself. You create, say, and show many things that reflect who you are. Yet everything you have ever created, said, and shown to the world is but a piece of your greatness. You are much more than they can see.

Me? I am the same, much more than you can see. More than you will ever know. It began with a bang — the big bang I created to give you a universe of beauty, order, and secrets beyond your understanding. Every seen and unseen thing in it is but a mere fraction of my greatness: every planet, every stone, every tree, every spider, every roar, and every smile.

I placed each drop of water in the oceans and I placed each tear in your eye. I made differences that make everyone the same, laughter that makes you cry, love that gives you pain, music that speaks to you, words unable to express your thoughts, colors beyond your sight, and death that brings forth new life. Above all things, I created you. I created you to be with me.

But you choose to know doubt, feel pain, have hunger, live hurt, confess frustration, act less than you are, and want more than enough. You need only me yet you deny me because I am beyond your reason.

If you have ever felt love, happiness, pain, or disappointment, I have felt these as well; your deepest emotion is a small degree of what I feel for you. I poured out my love for you. When you do wrong I grieve, because I know what I created you to be and what I created you to know.

Imagine, for a while, knowing joy, having hope, seeing love, being filled, and feeling free — completely, always, everywhere, abundantly, and forever!

Where you want to go, only I can take you. Who you want to be, only I can make you. What you want to see, only I can show you. What you want to know, only I can tell you - and I will, with a whisper, not a shout. The works of my hand speak loudly enough. Why aren't you listening?

I hear you. I see you. I know you. Yes, I planned you. I gave you choices. Please, give me a chance.

Choose me.

Dare me. Try me. Ask me. You can have and you will know.

I will forgive you. I will heal you. I will change you. I will consume you.

I already redeemed you. I sent a Savior to bridge the divide between you and me. He died and then He rose. No one else did. No one else could. I did it for you, because I love you.

I have true love for you because I am love, everlasting.

I am truth. I am peace. I am hope.

And, I am here, calling you. Now.

Answer me and answer to me, only.

For I am God.

ALONE.

PART TWO

EVERMORE

ENLIGHTENED

You ran into the Son and went home to tell others. In the light, you raised your hands and found me - right there next to you.

I'm right where I've been the entire time, in the shadows waiting for you. I am released and we are united. You wave to the sky. You laugh because I'm waving back at you.

Today, I'm more than a shadow. I'm your Spirit, the part of you that came alive when you embraced the light of His love. Together we're living and we'll be dancing forever in the sun.

ALONE

Breathe

I answered yes to You and I no longer wait for death. After living at the edge of breathing, my DNR is torn into leaves and flies into the rushing wind.

This wind, it carries the death of my last breath, while synchronizing the exhalations of every living thing You created. The wind is Your life-giving, life-sustaining breath of love, resuscitating my will to live. Breathe in me!

Today, I fight for life, and when the wind blows, in sweet irony, I taste my defeat. My every breath releases a part of my soul to commune with a multitude of other releases. And then my surrender returns to me and bores into my depths an overwhelming peace.

In my vanquished state, I behold the wind's breath-taking revelations of You: in the tales entertaining the birds to laughter; in the leaves waving ovations for the sun's symphony; in the centuries of hope sealed in an instant after a birthday wish; in the silence of the rain's approach; in the trumpeter's thought before he makes a sound; in the gasps of a woman giving birth; in the reverberation of a lost touch; in the divine aroma of every flower's heartbeat; and in the kiss of a child's breath, smoldering from the delicate explosion of Easter's last bubble.

Yes, I am ready to face death. But if there is the slightest chance to revive me, oh *come North wind, awaken! Come South wind, blow.* Breathe into me new life.

I know the years of my days are growing close to their end. At my final breath, the wind will whisper into my left ear echoes of yesterday's pain. For my right, it will conduct the angels' chimes for my last night's lullaby.

Upon waking, I will stand with You on the edge of heaven, against the rapid wind. I will be renewed. I will implode with both the memory and vision of eternity. There I will live with You and I will not be alone. And, I will breathe, forever.

BLINDED

In this new place, I found my home.

I've started going to a church where I've met people who enjoy spending time with orphans like me. They take me sightseeing and they have shown me things I never thought my eyes would see, like movies, the ocean, and myself on ice skates!

Because of them, I'm also learning about God, how He brought me here, and how He's watching over me. They're showing me how, beyond the pain on earth, there is a greater plan for us in heaven. I'm looking forward to heaven.

Every time I close my eyes, I see my father, my mother, and my brother. They're smiling at me and they're glad I'm seeing and doing all the things we dreamed about.

The people in this new place, they are my family now too. They don't have eyes like mine, but in theirs, I see only love!

That's good enough for me.

ALONE

CHANCE

I'm now a student of love.

There is so much to learn. I continue to study things; a conference or a book here or there. However, I participate with new eyes and a new heart. To me, these things serve as confirmations, not directions.

I look to Him for the answers I want. And He gives them to me — not always right away, but the answers are never late. Then, He answers questions I had never even thought to ask.

There is one path. Yes, it is narrow, but it's true. And I've got one life to live: this one.

Therefore I am to going to live it with all the passion, vigor, and joyful abandon I can muster — like it's my last chance, my only chance. And when I die, it will be forever. I'll be glad it's over too, because in the end, I will be with Him.

He knows it all and soon I will know complete love.

ALONE

DRUNK

Everybody needs something. And I like my coffee. It keeps me company. It's all I need and nothing else.

I'm not hurting anyone. I'm not a criminal. And it's not like I'm addicted to drugs, cigarettes, alcohol, pornography, shopping, or even food. Those are the real addicts. They spend insane amounts of money on their addictions everyday. They're the ones with the problem, not me. I'm not like them at all.

Besides, if I gave it up, what else what I do? What else is there to drink?

"If you knew the gift of God ... you would have asked him and he would have given you living water ... everyone who drinks this water will be thirsty again, but whoever drinks the water I give him will never thirst. Indeed the water I give him will become in him a spring of water welling up to eternal life."

John 4: 10, 13- 14
NIV

ALONE

FAT-FREE

You still think I'm fat. But the laugh's on and, yep, around me. There is plenty of me to go around, but there is much more inside you can't see. It's my big fat secret.

See, I'm fat on the outside and on the inside. There's so much joy in me, I'm fat to have somewhere to put it all. The joy inside is growing and I can't keep it in.

So I've started walking it out and off. The heat I generate when I walk is lighting up my own life. Walking is still work and I'm loving the job. While everyone else zips by, I take my time and enjoy the sights; I am fascinated at the sight of me falling more in love with Him as He leads me every step of the way.

It seems like I've been to a lot of places, traveling by foot. He's taken me to many places and shown me all kinds of things. And when I get home, He takes me straight to the mirror and shows me how I'm created in His image. There is more to me than meets the eyes! I've seen beyond my face. And I've moved past my maybes, and the butts, blocking your view of me.

Whether you see my shake as thin or thick, it doesn't matter. You see me and that's enough. Maybe one day you'll see where I'm going, and follow me.

ALONE

Cruising or crawling, I'm not alone. He's right here with me, and will be forever; right by my big phat side.

TEARS

Nu face come here. Long fuzz top of face. It pik me.

Ole face say nu face a Snug-ga-ler. Me close to nu face. Me warm.

Me wish no nooduls. Me want say to nu face, me air sad. Me stop air soon. Nu face see? Nu face rain ove me?

Me hope feel rain when stop air. Me glad face here. God sind nu face to rain ove wee me.

ALONE

GRAMPS

It's never too late to learn how to live. I learned in the nick of time.

People visit here a lot. There are groups and people by themselves hoping to hear a memory or two.

While I was sharing my memories, they were sharing God's love and teaching me how, at my age, I can find something to be glad about. There's a plan for me. The plan is not for me to find a way out of here, or how to get more out of my family, but a plan about how to find a new heart and a new joy.

I still don't see my grandkids as much as I would like, but these days, I'm making more memories, and more people are seeing my teeth. I'm getting my money's worth.

ALONE

OUTREACH

I live alone with my plants and with the birds who have chosen to build a nest outside my window. Most of all, Your presence keeps me company.

At home, I often find things breathing and changing. The other day, I looked over my shoulder and You gave me a little red flower blooming from the plant by the window. I didn't even know that plant could blossom.

I'm spending more of my time making new friends. There are a lot of people out there who don't have anyone else and they feel alone. Many people who are old, young, sick, or poor can use someone with the kind of time I have to give.

No, I don't watch as much TV as before. One night I woke up, and for a second the screen was dark, and I caught a reflection of myself. I turned off the set because I got tired of hiding in front in it, hiding from myself and from You.

My family and friends still bother me about settling down. Maybe one day I will. I'm looking forward to meeting someone with, more than anything, a heart like mine that burns with love for You. Then, I will gaze into eyes reflecting Your perfect and unconditional love for me. But if I don't ever settle down, that's okay too. I have already discovered my first love. And You are more than enough.

I'm answering my door a lot these days. Now, when someone knocks, I pull back the curtains and have a look outside, and while I'm at it, inside. I've seen a few false starts, but no false hopes.

As before, sounds are all around me. Life whirls outside. Those birds, they sing me a new song every morning. Like them, I awake every morning with a song in my heart. I sing of assurance, joy and peace – and of how I am falling more in love with You each day.

Extraordinary

I found my passion and my calling. I am making a difference in the world by making a difference in the lives of those who depend on me. I don't have fame or a fortune, my life is what it is and I am where I am, yet every day is an opportunity to go beyond average. I do have a calling.

I heard You calling me to be more than the average husband. I was called to honor my wife, to protect her, to caress her, and show her my strength by being gentle. I have been called to put her needs above mine, and to do what I can to support her and her dreams. My calling is to listen to her without distraction, to compliment her without fail, and to bring home to her more than bread for dinner. I am to bring home my soul - wide open and unmasked for *only her* to know.

I heard You calling me to be more than the average father. I was called to be a leader and to teach my kids how to live a life of integrity and dignity. I have been called to model for them how to respect themselves, each other, their elders, and those in authority. My calling is to give them my hugs, my patience, and my approval. They look up to me, so to do my best, I will look up to You.

I heard you calling me to be more than the average man. I have been called to treat everyone with respect whether they report to me, work alongside me, or I report to them. In return, You give me the wisdom to make the difficult decisions and the strength to be a man of my word and Yours.

Yes, I found my passion. I heard my calling and I am awed at the privilege to answer it.

LIGHT

I'm black.

I stand out. I'm the spot in the crowd, but not for long. With each handshake, every kiss, and every birth, He's merging us into one exquisite race. Everyone will speak the same language again, and we will be the same, each one of us, painted in the color of love.

In the meantime, since everyone spots me, I will give them something to see. His love's light will shine through me, right there, in the darkness.

That will show them.

ALONE

Full

With so many kids, our house buzzes and there's lots to do. Sometimes I get lost in the shuffle. These kids are all ours and all our own.

They were destined for us, but our hearts were broken. Our hearts were too broken to see that, all along, He had planned to fill the cracks with pieces of love that others left behind.

I'll tell you more about our full house later but I have to go now. I'm taking the kids ice skating again. But first, I've got to find my keys....

ALONE

RESTING

Boys will be boys.

And we'll be alright even though there's no man around yet.
Thank goodness there's a man above taking care of us.

ALONE

ONE

We got tired of being alone together. We went far away, ran into You, and found each other.

"I will give up everything for you."
"I will give in to you."

"I appreciate you."
"I accept you."

"I will be weak before you."
"When you are weak, you are strong."

"I will learn you."
"I will support you in everything, always."

"I see myself in you."
"I like what I see."

"I will touch you with more than my hands."
"I will embrace you with more than my arms."

"You are my jewel."
"You are my hero."

"I want you."
"I need you."

"In you, I find the missing part of me."
"In me, there is only you."

"One can be made of two"
"We two are one."

We are together now.   Soon there will be a third. We will all be together, strong and one.

BEGGAR

Everywhere is my home, so my window to the world is open.

I am poor, yet I live in paradise. I'm outside where I can see everything. I can feel everything: the wind, the rain, and the sun. My life is really living.

Someone pointed me to a man and a kitchen called the Bread of Life. I go there everyday to have good home-cooked meals. And when I'm done eating, they let me mop the floors! It makes me happy and it's the least I can do in return for the full stomach they give me.

On the shelves there, they offer me all the bread I can take with me — free. Every day the shelves are overflowing so I'm never hungry. I don't have to chase squirrels anymore. I take some of the bread loaves down with me to my bed of rocks in the creek. Sometimes I use a loaf as a pillow, to help me sleep.

When I'm lying there in the creek, the water sounds like a little fountain — the electric kind with rocks I've seen people throwing out when they stop working. Those fountains look like they used to be at somebody's desk someplace up high. I've heard about some people paying to camp out in the open like I do. A lot of people trying to create up there what I got down here.

I don't have anything, and no thing has me. I am free to go where He wants to send me, be what He wants to make me, and to do what He asks of me. And what I do is beg for more of Him everyday. For Him to keep me poor, keep me needing Him, so that I know He's all I need. I guess that makes me a beggar.

I'm homeless, I've just a few clothes, and I've barely got shoes. But it is well with my soul.

ANGEL

I take out trash. I leave the offices nice and clean.

Most people still don't see me, and they still don't know who I am. That's okay because I know there is someone up there who knows my name, even though everybody down here seems more important than me.

Everyone else skips to meetings and hurries about. Other than vacuum and empty trash, there's not a whole lot for me to do, especially in some of those big offices. It seems like those folks have the most space and the least things.

So even though they may not know who I am, I leave my prayers in their offices, just so there's something else in there keeping them company.

ALONE

OUTLOOK

I'm still standing.

I'm doing the best I can to protect. My job is to make things secure, not people.

I continue to spend most nights here reading, thinking, and wondering, most of the time, about You and how You promised You'd be up there — looking down and watching over me while I'm looking out.

ALONE

HEADIN'

Drivin' trucks is my life. It's a good livin' and it takes me places. Since I met Him, I've started takin' it all in.

The cows, sheep, and horses, they look fed, taken care of, and at peace. The sunsets and sunrises are rare life-size paintin's. There's an artist up there, creatin' a new picture for me every day. And the flowers in the fields along the highway are a bunch of lil' faces smilin' and wavin' at me as I truck by.

There are plenty of things to look at and to look for on days when I can take my time drivin'. I even found myself glancin' at the road in my rear-view mirror. I saw the reflection of the road in my right eye as I looked in that mirror. Next, I saw the rear-view mirror's picture of the road in my eye. Then I was left, lookin' for my eye in my eyes' reflection of the rear-view.

I kept lookin' for the road deep in my rear-view mirror because for the first time, I was seein' myself leave the past behind.

This time, I'm headin' home.

ALONE

WATERBORNE

I wanted to fly. I did not find wings jumping from high, so I went for a dive down below.

SCUBA-ed from head-to-toe, I dove into the ocean, flying downwards, falling free. For the very first time in my waking life, there was no sky. And there was no need for wings. Falling further, I suspended my concept of time to memorize the feeling of my descent. And for a short while, I existed in an unknown interval — I did not know what was around me or what awaited below, and I did not know if I was going to reach the bottom or how far down I went. My eyes were open but I did not see. There was light floating around me, then darkness, then light again. The ocean's depth opened to me and I was stunned. I had experienced a reverse birth.

Diving like flying, should never be attempted alone. An experienced diving partner took me along to explore the underworld. I have heard that the earth is seventy-percent water, and that I too am made of at least seventy-percent water. I suppose if I ran through the depths of every valley and danced across the peaks of every mountain, I would experience a mere thirty-percent of the earth's majesty — and less than a third of me would virtually incorporate it. My solo flight attempt provided no answer, so I hoped here, underneath it all with my guide, the enigmatic seventy-percent of the physical world would be revealed.

When I reached the bottom of the sea, my partner was waiting for me and took my hand. Underwater, we were transformed into fraternal twins waiting to be born. Being the elder, with amazing pride and grace, he led me on a tour of our inside: gesturing at fish, teasing me with crabs, showing me sea anemones. It was as if he himself created everything around us, and he was excited to see my reaction to his ingenious creations living below. Everywhere, swaying in filtered green hues, I saw groves of red algae hula and kiss us hello as we toured along.

Diving with SCUBA, my sensory expression was displaced. I had a voice, but I was unable to speak. I had a nose, but I was unable to smell. Because I wore gloves, I had hands that could touch, but were unable to feel. Eventually, the pace of my heart spoke the unspoken words, ingested the unaired aromas and converged with each organism's warmth. I had eyes but they were paralyzed with awe and even though they saw the miracle of how the ocean consumed me, they could not find the tears to cry.

With fraught, I searched within for my tears but found them swimming outside and around me, communing with a global array of other tears. Tears of joy, relief, hope, anger, laughter, pain, frustration, passion, fear, sadness, and love which I thought had dissolved during their facial descents had, in truth, been gathering here. They had rematerialized as the ocean, and they engulfed me. Astonished, I moved a little slower, placed my muted ear to the water, and I steadied my breathing. The roar was barely audible but I heard it: the enormous, harmonious sound of everyone crying.

To get my bearings in the ocean, I had to swim looking downwards. In doing so, I was amazed when I thought I saw the ocean's floor twinkling. When my eyes adjusted, I saw there was indeed still a sky and I had found it — here at my feet! In stark realization of my world's inversion, my hand at once reached for the millions of stars shining so brightly in water's daylight. For that moment, the sky ran through my encased fingers and I was touching heaven.

A newborn diver, I had trouble swimming with fins and much of my time underwater was spent on my knees — yes, crawling across the heavens. The surge of the ocean moved me perpendicular to the direction I was moving. Just as I felt I was about to be swept off course, the surge balanced me in the other direction. After a few more repetitions of the surge's sway, I gave in, felt cradled and wanted to fall asleep. Almost relaxed, I felt the rhythm of the sea. The liquid serenity reminded me of lying down on the grass and looking up at the clouds gliding in their silent reverie. I see the earth turning, while I'm reclining in the rush of life. Maybe if I let go when I return to the surface, I will feel that the land longs, like the sea, to cradle me and rock me into soft slumber.

Moving along, I encountered a bashful water-colored fish who was so gorgeous that I, at once remembering that fish do not have mirrors, invited him to look at his reflection through my eyes. But to him I was a stranger. He didn't know me well enough to trust the image my eyes would emulate.

Next, I saw two red-orange starfish with their arms so tightly clenched they looked like disembodied fingers fused together. I wondered how and why they became so inseparable. With a questioning finger, I touched them to see if they were in reality one organism. My touch confirmed that they were two and one. Twins, also waiting to be born, they had folded themselves together to share the same strand of nourishment.

I emerged from the amniotic sea of emotions. I was exhausted, heavy, and ravenous. There were many people up above at the edge of the shore taking in the view. They looked like they were waiting for me. Like a beacon of love, one woman was smiling and waving to the others out in the water. I focused on her and struggled to the shore, every pore drowned with the residue of innumerable tears and my mouth filled with little stars from heaven's floor. When I came to rest on-shore, I saw a promise swelling inside of the welcoming woman. Pregnant, she was the most exquisite sight surfacing above the horizontal that divided the two skies. There, wrapped up in the view of her living in the sun, the seventy percent mystery of the physical world unveiled itself before me.

Yes, I wanted to fly. I almost died trying. But by stepping into the water, I was baptized: I died and then I was reborn — born again.

FOUND

For many years, I tried. I looked around and saw mere faces: fleeting emotions ticking on every wall, myriad moods masking desperate attempts, and painted realities bearing no resemblance to the truth. I looked behind and saw stone images: grey footprints cemented on shaded paths, resounding silences that should have spoken, and quivering rocks releasing tears of my regret. I looked at me and saw a mirror of darkness: abysmal ignorance poised against itself, unconscious dreams deprived of morning, and vain achievements signifying nothing.

One day, I retreated. I dared back to my core, looked deeper within it, and, this time, I saw a vortex of light emerge. The light was nurturing my every breath, freeing the reflections of my fears, and revealing my destiny in a clear vision that blinded me. I saw hope stirring in its womb while death was fighting in its grave. I saw tomorrow's joy whispering sweet nothings to shadows of yesterday's sorrow. Illuminated, I saw, within, reason surrendering to knowing.

In one moment, I understood. I looked and saw how it was You I was hiding from and looking for all along. You were there at my core, asking me to see You, and then see myself revealed in You. Why was I so afraid? Maybe I was scared because surrender meant You were greater than me. Surrender meant accepting I wasn't strong enough, smart enough, or brave enough.

My insufficiency scared me then. Today, my limitations are the cornerstone of my peace. I embrace that I am not enough; I don't ever have to be enough, because You are. When You found me in that place, my hiding and searching ended — and the journey began.

Now, everyday I see every thing. Forever, I am everything in You, including lost.

Never, will I be alone.

AFTERWORD

EVERLASTING

CHANGE

Maybe you've seen yourself in one of the chapters of this book, maybe you haven't. Whichever, I am certain you have felt alone and at times wondered about there being more to life than immediate living and dying. I have. We all have because God placed the yearning for truth and intimacy in each of our hearts — a void leading us to look for Him, to Him, and to find fulfillment in Him alone.

Your life may be desperate, it may be great, or it might be just okay. (Just okay?!) Even if you think you've got it all, why not ask for more? I believe if we ask for more than what we've been living, by bringing heaven into each of our hearts, we will experience heaven right here on earth. There is only ONE way that gives us the power to fulfill this vision and that is through Jesus Christ. Jesus Himself made that claim.* Given His life, He was more than a prophet. He was either outright insane or divinely heaven-sent. **You decide.**

If you have felt Him knocking at your heart, in the form of a laugh, a tear, or an eerie relevance as you read the stories in ALONE, I invite you to answer the door by repeating this simple ABC prayer:

> *God, sin is anything that separates me from You. Right here and now:*
> † *I Admit that I am a sinner and that I have sinned.*
> † *I Believe that Christ died and rose to redeem me.*
> † *I Confess Jesus as my Savior and ask you to come into my life so that I will never be alone.*

That's it. It's not about rules or rituals, but about relationship. It's between you and Him, no one else. But allow me to add, having

---

* *"I am the way and the truth and the life. No one comes to the Father except through me."*

John 14:6
NIV

lived much of ALONE before and after the title chapter, I myself am living proof of His constant, life-changing, and, more importantly, *heart-changing* power. Simply ask anyone who knew me before.

I prayed the above prayer in my youth, but it wasn't until three years ago when I went beyond basic acceptance of Christ and cried out to God to take my filthy life, with all of its restless mediocrity, and cleanse it, and endow me with a divine purpose. I said to my Creator that if He assigned each planet its own path in the universe, then surely He designed mere me with a unique journey as well. I asked Him to reveal it to me. I pleaded for Him to break me and fill me with hope, wisdom, and peace. Like the birds outside my window, I too wanted to rise every morning with a song in my heart rather than an expletive on my lips. With my face buried in my need for change, I asked Him to reveal Himself to me in everything, and for Him to give me the new eyes and heart of a child. I begged Him to revive me, possess me, and become the one true and faithful lover of my soul.

Tired and spent of forging my own successes, and finding dead, superficial satisfaction after accomplishing the goals I had set for myself, I decided to go beyond acceptance to unequivocal surrender. And guess what? In response to my plea for a fulfilling life and a renewed heart, God said "*Yes, I will give you these and, in time, more. Just stay close and walk with Me.*"

Let me not mislead you, my life is far from perfect. However, since I made the decision to give my entire self to Him, my bad days with Him are infinitely better than my best days without Him. I continue with struggles every day, including bouts of self-pity and frustration. But through them, I am learning to press into Him, and I see my struggles being transformed into victories. Sometimes the transformation happens slower than I expect, but there is change, deep and lasting. I need not look to anyone else. I thirst for nothing else: nothing else.

And every so often, when I am thanking God or admiring the simple beauty of the day, He blesses me with a glimpse of the depth and sheer purity of His love for me, and for you. In that moment, my heart opens wide and I see mercy, I feel peace, and I am left sweetly consumed, uncontrollably trembling, and utterly breathless in a pool of my own rainbow-filled tears, awed by His gentle loving-kindness. I have had only a few experiences like these, but they have been enough to give me overwhelming reason to believe, to trust, and to proclaim the thunder of His power and the ocean of His love. He is real!

For me, experiencing God is like when I dare to stare without end into the brightest noon sun. I want to see more than the sun's rays, I want to see to the center of its light, but I cannot stare for any prolonged length of time because the sun is too bright and the light is too painful for my eyes.

Similarly, my heart wants to remain forever unshielded in the glimpse of God's love but, because of my fragile humanity, I cannot. His love is more than me, much more. I could travel to the sun, go beyond every star, and visit galaxies far away, yet with my fallible human mind, I will *never* see or understand how God's love came to be. I will never know. And even if I traveled to the ends of being and reason, it would not matter, because in the abyss of my soul, I feel Him here — inside of me, waiting, watching, and loving me. So until the time when the sun ceases to set, and I can bask, bare in the eternity of His love's healing warmth, my days will be spent sharing the message of His beauty and sacrifice.

Please choose the Lord, invite him into your life by accepting the sacrifice of His son Jesus. You will be blessed beyond measure, and beyond temporal things, with the ultimate gift of seeing and growing closer to Him every day. NOTHING compares to experiencing God and observing His work within you.

If you do not believe there is a God who is Father and Creator, take a few minutes and ask yourself why. For a sober moment, put aside everything you have been taught, what you think, and what you have believed thus far. From within your heart, ask yourself why, and write down three reasons why you do not believe. Then ask that paper, the wall, or the table, that, if there is a God, may He open your eyes and heart for you to see Him. Expect to be shown, whether it is in the starry beauty of a child's freckles, in the statistically improbable order of the universe, or in the chaos of your own life.

Ask God, if He is there, to reveal His love for you in a specific way that *you* can understand and accept. He will because your

Creator craves to be with you, one-on-one. You need only ask and receive Him.

When God shows you Himself, do not hesitate. Go to Him. Forget about the barriers of your past, other people, or other reasons that have held you back. His heart aches for you and everyone who lives apart from Him. Did you know the angels rejoice whenever someone comes to abide in His light? God waits for you with outstretched hands that are indeed big enough to hold the universe, remove your doubts, and change your heart. When you see Him, go to Him that very second, just as you are presently. His everlasting love will even meet you halfway and do the rest.

God bless you and may eternal peace be yours. — WMT

ALONE

ORDER FORM

Complete the form below to request additional copies.
Please print legibly

Name: _____

Address #1: _____

Address #2: _____

City: _____ State/Province:_____

Postal/Zip Code: _____ Country: _____

Phone: _____

Email: _____

Up to 3 complimentary copies, postage waived, will be sent to the above address while publisher supplies last. For bulk quantities, send request to email below.

Number of Copies # _____

If you are interested in sending a tax-deductible donation with your request, please make check payable to Abundant Life Christian Fellowship, Building Fund (or ALCF Building Fund). Visit www.alcf.net .

Mail to: Never Alone 139, P.O. Box 50054, Palo Alto, CA 94303 USA
Email: NeverAlone139@aol.com

2513-SK